D0975607

MEET BATMAN

SCHOLASTIC

MEET BATMAN

WRITTEN BY QUINLAN B. LEE   ILLUSTRATED BY DAVE WHITE
BATMAN CREATED BY BOB KANE

ISBN 978-0-545-55240-0

12 11   16 17 18 19/0

Printed in Malaysia   106

First printing, January 2014

What is **that** in the sky?
It is a **flash**!
It is a **bat**!

We need the **man** in the **mask**. We need **Batman**!

Batman jumps
in the Batmobile.
He needs a **plan**.
He needs to get
to his **lab**.
Fast!

Batman's lab is in
a cave.
The Batcave is where
he makes **plans**.
He **plans** to **catch** the
bad guys.

Batman needs help. He **asks** Robin to help make a **plan**. He is **Batman's** right-**hand man**.

Batman needs to go **fast**!
He has a Batboat.
It is **fast**!
He has a Batcycle.
It is **fast**!
He has a Batplane.
It is a **blast**!

Batman has a **plan**.
He puts a **map**
in the Batplane.
He puts some **traps**
in the Batplane.
He puts some . . .

Snacks in the Batplane!
Yum! **Batman** loves
PB and **Jam**.
Now, **that** is a **plan**!

DC UNIVERSE
SUPER HEROES

PHONICS
BOOK 2 · SHORT E

GET THAT CAT!

WRITTEN BY QUINLAN B. LEE   ILLUSTRATED BY DAVE WHITE
BATMAN CREATED BY BOB KANE

ISBN 978-0-545-55241-7

12 11   16 17 18 19/0

Printed in Malaysia   106

First printing, January 2014

"**Help**!" a man **yells**. Catwoman has a **gem**. Quick! **Get help**!

"Meow! Come here, my **pet**," she says. Catwoman is **set** to **get** away.

She **jets** to the right.
CRASH!
She **jets** to the **left**.
CRASH!
What a **mess**!

Who can **help**?
Quick!
Before she **gets** away
with the **gem**.

Batman **jets** in.
"**Help** is here!" he **yells**.
"Come here, my **pet**."

The rope makes a **net**.
Get set to **get wet**,
Catwoman!

What a **mess**!
"Meow! Cats do not like
to **get wet**,"
says Catwoman.

"I **bet** you will be
nice and dry . . .
in your **cell**!" Batman
tells her.

Catwoman is **set** to **get** away with a **gem** that is not hers. Who can **help**?

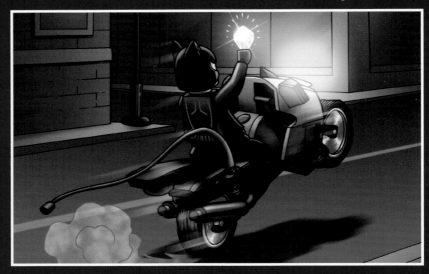

In this book you will practice these **short E** words:

bet	jets	set
cell	left	tells
gem	mess	wet
get	net	yells
help	pet	

978-0-545-55241-7

LEGO

DC UNIVERSE™

SUPER HEROES

PHONICS
BOOK 3 · SHORT I

COME QUICK!

SCHOLASTIC

COME QUICK!

WRITTEN BY QUINLAN B. LEE　　**ILLUSTRATED BY DAVE WHITE**

ISBN 978-0-545-55242-4

FSC
www.fsc.org
MIX
Paper from
responsible sources
FSC® C101773

12 11　　　　16 17 18 19/0

Printed in Malaysia　　　106

First printing, January 2014

Superman hears Batman
from far away.
Batman says,
"Come **quick**!"
"**Quick** is what I do best!"
the Flash says.
"I **will** be there **in** a flash!"

The Flash gets
to the spot.
There is just a **big hill**
of **bricks**.
"Why **did** Batman say
to come **quick**?"

Next Superman comes.
"Out of the way," he says.
"These **bricks** need a
quick fix!"

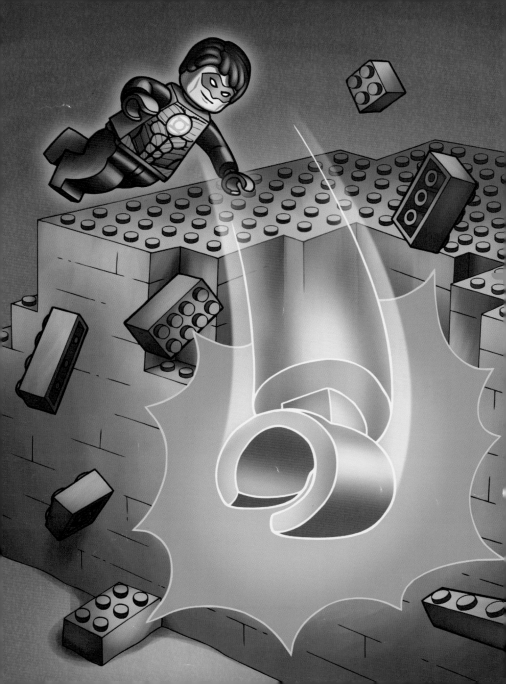

Then Green Lantern comes.

"I came **quick**. But what is **this**?" he asks.

"**Bricks**," says the Flash.

"We can **hit** these **bricks**!" Green Lantern says.

Then Wonder Woman comes.
"Out of the way," she says. "Batman needs us!"
She makes a **fist**.
She **spins** and **spins**.
Then she **hits** the **bricks**.

WHAM!
The last of the **bricks**
fall down!

"Just **in** the **nick** of time!"
says Batman.
"The fire is **still** hot!"
"**Sit**! Grab a **stick**,"
says Robin.
Superman asks, "**This** is
why we came so **quick**?"

"Yes! Now we can **sit** back and relax," says Batman.

Batman is stuck under a **hill** of **bricks**.
His friends **will** help and **quick**!

In this book you will practice these **short I** words:

big	hit	stick
bricks	in	still
did	nick	this
fist	quick	will
fix	sit	
hill	spins	

978-0-545-55242-4

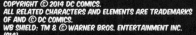

LEGO

DC UNIVERSE™

SUPER HEROES

PHONICS
BOOK 4 • SHORT O

STOP THE BOT

SCHOLASTIC

PHONICS
BOOK 4 · SHORT O

STOP THE BOT!

WRITTEN BY QUINLAN B. LEE   ILLUSTRATED BY DAVE WHITE

SUPERMAN CREATED BY JERRY SIEGEL AND JOE SHUSTER
BY SPECIAL ARRANGEMENT WITH THE JERRY SIEGEL FAMILY

ISBN 978-0-545-55243-1

12 11   16 17 18 19/0

Printed in Malaysia   106

First printing, January 2014

STOMP! STOMP! STOMP!
Lex has a big **robot**.
The **bot** has **got**
Wonder Woman.

Who will **stop** the **bot**?
Is it a bird? **NOT**!
Is it a plane? **NOT**!

It is Superman!
Lex takes a **shot**.
Superman **drops**
like a **rock**.

Now who can **stop**
Lex and his **bot**?

Not so fast!
Wonder Woman **rocks**
and **socks** the **bot**.
Lex yells, "**Stop**!"

What is that?
Is it **fog**? **NOT**!
Is it **smog**? **NOT**!
It is Superman's
ice breath.

The **bot locks**.
The **bot rocks**.
The **bot drops**!
Lex's plan **flops**!

Who can **stop** the **bot**?
Superman and
Wonder Woman
can **stop** the **bot**!

Who will **stop** Lex and his **bot**?
Superman will **stomp** that **bot**!

In this book you will practice these **short O** words:

bot	locks	smog
drops	not	socks
flops	robot	stomp
fog	rock	stop
got	shot	

UP, UP, AND AWAY

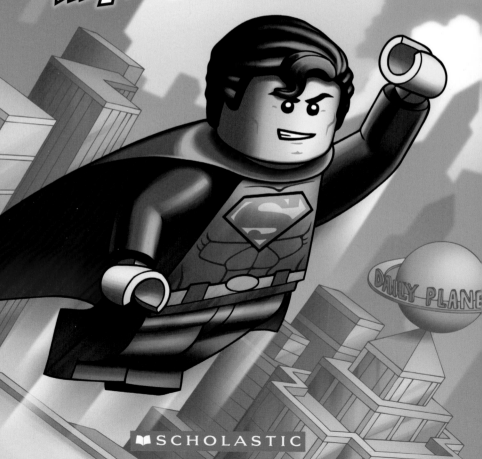

DAILY PLANE

SCHOLASTIC

DC UNIVERSE

SUPER HEROES

PHONICS
BOOK 5 · SHORT u

UP, UP, AND AWAY

WRITTEN BY QUINLAN B. LEE   ILLUSTRATED BY DAVE WHITE

SUPERMAN CREATED BY JERRY SIEGEL AND JOE SHUSTER
BY SPECIAL ARRANGEMENT WITH THE JERRY SIEGEL FAMILY

ISBN 978-0-545-55244-8

12 11   16 17 18 19/0

Printed in Malaysia   106

First printing, January 2014

This is Superman.
He can **run** fast!
He can **jump** high!
He can do **much** more
than any man!

The **sun** makes
Superman strong.
He can pick **up**
a **bus** so it does
not get **crushed**.

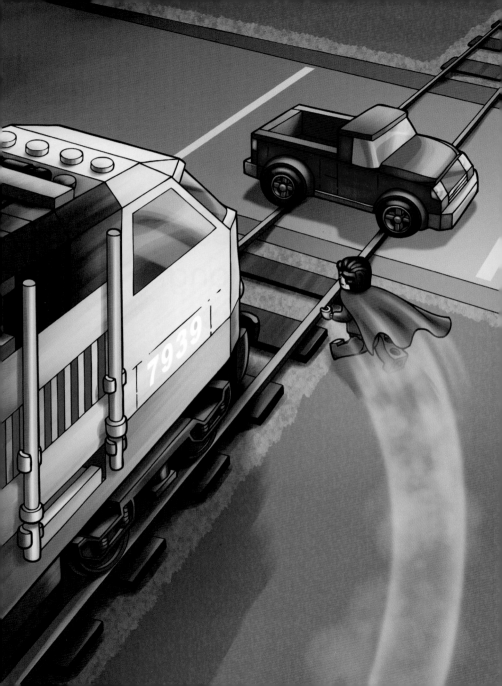

The **sun** makes
Superman fast.
He can **run much** faster
than a train.
He can **run** so fast
he can save the
truck just in time!

Superman can **jump**
as high as the sky.
Superman can **jump**
as high as the **sun**.
He can **jump up**, **up**, **up**.
Then he can fly away!

Superman can see through walls. Superman can hear anything, even a little **hush**.

Superman can **huff**.
He can **puff**.
He can **huff** and **puff**
a big **gust** of cold air.

Superman also likes to have **fun**.
He likes to **run** and **jump** with his friends.

Sometimes he
has too **much fun**
in the **sun**!

The **sun** powers Superman so he can **huff**, **puff**, **jump** high, and lift a **bus**.

In this book you will practice these **short U** words:

bus	gust	run
crush	jump	sun
fun	just	truck
huff	much	up
hush	puff	

978-0-545-55244-8

 LEGO, THE LEGO LOGO, THE BRICK AND KNOB CONFIGURATIONS AND THE MINIFIGURE ARE TRADEMARKS OF THE LEGO GROUP. © 2014 THE LEGO GROUP. PRODUCED BY SCHOLASTIC INC. UNDER LICENSE FROM THE LEGO GROUP. PUBLISHED BY SCHOLASTIC INC.

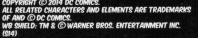

LEGO®

DC UNIVERSE™

SUPER HEROES

PHONICS
BOOK 6 · LONG A

TWO-FACE CHASE

SCHOLASTIC

DC UNIVERSE™

SUPER HEROES

PHONICS
BOOK 6 · LONG A

TWO-FACE CHASE

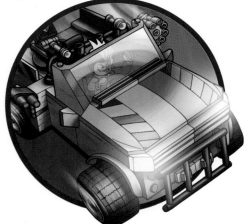

WRITTEN BY QUINLAN B. LEE   ILLUSTRATED BY DAVE WHITE

BATMAN CREATED BY BOB KANE

ISBN 978-0-545-55245-5

LEGO, the LEGO logo, the Brick and Knob configurations and the Minifigure are trademarks of the LEGO Group. © 2014 The LEGO Group. Produced by Scholastic Inc. under license from the LEGO Group.

Copyright © 2014 DC Comics.
All related characters and elements are trademarks of and © DC Comics.
(s14)

12 11   16 17 18 19/0

Printed in Malaysia   106

First printing, January 2014

Batman **races**
to the bank!
There is a **crane**
in the way.
He hits the **brakes**!
"I **hate** to be **late**!"
Batman yells.

Two-**Face** is in the **crane**.
He **makes** the bank
shake and **quake**.

The **crane makes**
a big hole!
Two-**Face takes** the **safe!**
"Now I will be really **late!**"
says Batman.
The **chase** is on!

Two-**Face races** away.
Batman **races** after him.
Two-**Face fakes** this way.
He **fakes** that way.
But he cannot **shake** Batman.

Two-**Face** does not see the end of the **lane**. He hits the **brakes**! Watch the **safe**!

"I'll **take** that **safe**,"
says Batman.
"I also have a **crane**,
Two-**Face**."

"I am sorry that I am **late**," says Batman. "I **came** to put money in your **safe**."

"But I had to **chase** the **safe** first!"

Batman is **late** to stop Two-**Face** as he **takes** the **safe**. Now there is a **chase**!

In this book you will practice these **long A** words:

brakes	fakes	quake
came	hate	races
crane	lane	safe
chase	late	shake
face	makes	take

978-0-545-55245-5

DC UNIVERSE™
SUPER HEROES

PHONICS
BOOK 7 · LONG E

MR. FREEZE

WRITTEN BY QUINLAN B. LEE   ILLUSTRATED BY DAVE WHITE
BATMAN CREATED BY BOB KANE

ISBN 978-0-545-55246-2

LEGO, the LEGO logo, the Brick and Knob configurations and the Minifigure are trademarks of the LEGO Group. © 2014 The LEGO Group.
Produced by Scholastic Inc. under license from the LEGO Group.

12 11   16 17 18 19/0

Printed in Malaysia   106

First printing, January 2014

Batman and Robin are in the Batboat.
"I **feel** the **need**!
I **feel** the **need** for **speed**!" says Robin.

Then a cold **breeze** blows.
Sleet falls down.
The Batboat hits ice!
It is stuck!

"We will **freeze**!"
says Robin.
"I **feel** the **need**!
I **feel** the **need** for . . .
skis!" says Batman.
"Now we can **keep** up
the **speed**!"

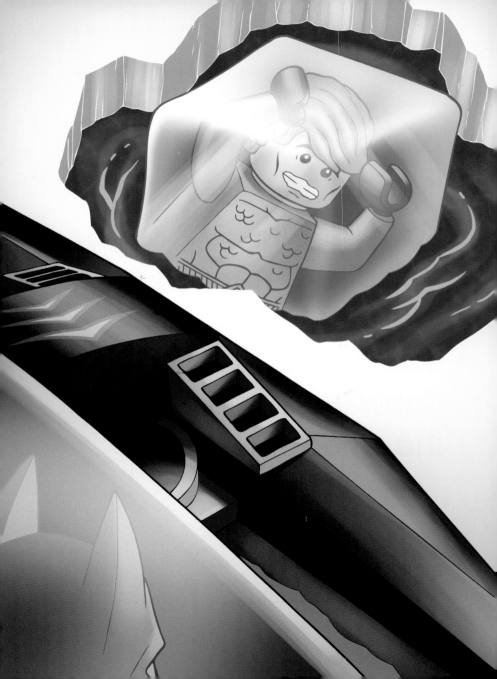

"Look!" yells Robin.
"Do you **see** what I **see**?"
"Yes!" Batman says.
"I **see** Aquaman. He is
deep in the ice."

"Yes, **indeed**," says
Mr. **Freeze**.
"Aquaman is in a
deep freeze.
I like my fish on ice."

Mr. **Freeze speeds** away!
The lake is a **sheet** of ice.
More **sleet** blows.
Batman and Robin
speed after him.
"Do you **see** Mr. **Freeze**?"
asks Batman.

"I **see** him!" says Robin.
"We **meet** again!"
Mr. **Freeze** says.
"Good. I like bats
and birds on ice, too.
Tweet! Tweet!"

"**Meet** this!" yells Batman.
"I like my ice in my
drinks and my friends
to be **free**!"

Mr. **Freeze** has Aquaman.
Batman **speeds** to **meet** his friend in **need**.

In this book you will practice these **long E** words:

breeze	indeed	sheet
deep	keep	sleet
feel	meet	speed
free	need	tweet
freeze	see	

978-0-545-55246-2

WWW.SCHOLASTIC.COM

RIDE ON!

PHONICS
BOOK 8 · LONG I

WRITTEN BY QUINLAN B. LEE   ILLUSTRATED BY DAVE WHITE

ISBN 978-0-545-55247-9

12 11   16 17 18 19/0

Printed in Malaysia   106

First printing, January 2014

FSC
www.fsc.org
MIX
Paper from
responsible sources
FSC® C101773

"You cannot **hide** this **time**, Bane," says Batman.
A **bike rides** by in the dark.
Is it Bane?

It is Catwoman!
She **smiles**.
"Are you looking for me?"
she says.
"I will not **hide** this **time**."

"You again?"
says Batman.
"You must have
nine lives.
Go play with some **mice**."
Another **bike rides** by in
the dark.
Is it Bane?

It is Poison **Ivy**!
She **smiles**.
"**Nice** to see you,"
she says.
"I will not **hide** this **time**."

"You again?"
says Batman.
"You are **like** a weed
that will not **die**.
Go climb a **pipe**!"
A tank **drives** by.
Is it Bane?

It is Bane!
Batman **flies** in the
skies after him.
Bane **drives**
fast, fast, faster!

Bane **drives** too fast.
Look out!
He **slides** into the **bikes**.
CRASH! POW!
WIPE OUT!

Now Batman **smiles**.
"Thanks, girls!" he says.
"This **time** you were on
my **side**."

Bane **drives** a tank on the **side** of the road.
It is **time** Batman used his own **ride** to catch him.

In this book you will practice these **long I** words:

bike	lives	skies
die	mice	slides
drives	nice	smiles
flies	nine	time
hide	pipe	wipe
ivy	ride	
like	side	

978-0-545-55247-9

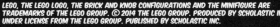

PHONICS
BOOK 9 · LONG O

NO JOKE!

WRITTEN BY QUINLAN B. LEE   ILLUSTRATED BY DAVE WHITE

ISBN 978-0-545-55248-6

12 11   16 17 18 19/0

Printed in Malaysia   106

First printing, January 2014

All of Gotham City is at **home** in bed.
No one is out.
Except one **lone** man . . .

The **Joker**!
"This **smoke** will help
you sleep . . . forever!"
he yells.
"And that is **no joke**."

Batman flies in.
"You **spoke** too soon,"
he says.
"Not all of Gotham City
is at **home, Joker**!"

"I'm sorry if I **woke** you up," the **Joker** says. "Nice **robe**— I mean cape. Did you leave your teddy bear at **home**?"

"Nice **rope**," says Batman. "I'd be sorry if it **broke, Joker.** I **hope** you can hang on."

Batman cuts the **rope**.
The **Joker** falls down
in the **smoke**.
He **chokes** and **chokes**
and **chokes**.
And then . . .

. . . ZZZZZzzzzzz.
"I **hope** you sleep
a long, long time,"
Batman tells him.
"And that's **no joke**."

"Does anyone have a
robe and teddy bear
for the **Joker**?"

The **Joker** has a **smoke joke** for the city.
We **hope** Batman can stop him.

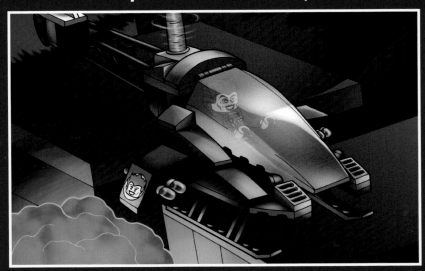

In this book you will practice these **long O** words:

broke	joke	rope
choke	Joker	smoke
home	lone	spoke
hope	robe	woke

978-0-545-55248-6

WWW.SCHOLASTIC.COM

LEGO

DC UNIVERSE™

SUPER HEROES

PHONICS
BOOK 10 • LONG U

GET A CLUE!

SCHOLASTIC

PHONICS
BOOK 10 · LONG U

GET A CLUE!

WRITTEN BY QUINLAN B. LEE   **ILLUSTRATED BY DAVE WHITE**

ISBN 978-0-545-55249-3

LEGO, the LEGO logo, the Brick and Knob configurations and the Minifigure are trademarks of the LEGO Group. © 2014 The LEGO Group. Produced by Scholastic Inc. under license from the LEGO Group.

Copyright © 2014 DC Comics.
All related characters and elements are trademarks of and © DC Comics.
(s14)

12 11   16 17 18 19/0

Printed in Malaysia   106

First printing, January 2014

FSC
www.fsc.org
MIX
Paper from
responsible sources
FSC® C101773

Batman gets a note.
It says: "I have the
guy in **blue**.
Do you want him back?
You know what to do.
Look for me
and get my **clues**."

"Guy in **blue**?
Who could it be?"
asks Robin.
"We could use more
clues."

The note says:
Try to **use** another **clue**.
Blue-boy thinks he's
super when he flies.
But a bit of Kryptonite
makes him dive."

"He has Superman!"
Batman says.
"But where is he?"
"We could still **use** more
clues!" Robin tells him.

The Riddler has
another **clue**:
"Still stuck?
Superman is, too!
You are late.
You are being **rude**.
Find the time, you will
find the **glue**."
"I get that **clue**!"
says Batman.
"Let's go!"

"I could **use** a hand!" says Superman. "What **glue** did the Riddler **use**?" asks Robin. "It is Kryptonite **glue**," Batman says.

Batman and Robin **use** the crane to pull Superman from the **glue**.
"Thanks," he tells them. "You are **true** friends."

"You are **rude**
to tie up this **dude**,"
says the Riddler.
"Now I have the **blues**."

Batman must **use** the **clues** to save his **true blue** friend.

In this book you will practice these **long U** words:

blue	glue	use
clue	rude	
dude	true	

978-0-545-55249-3